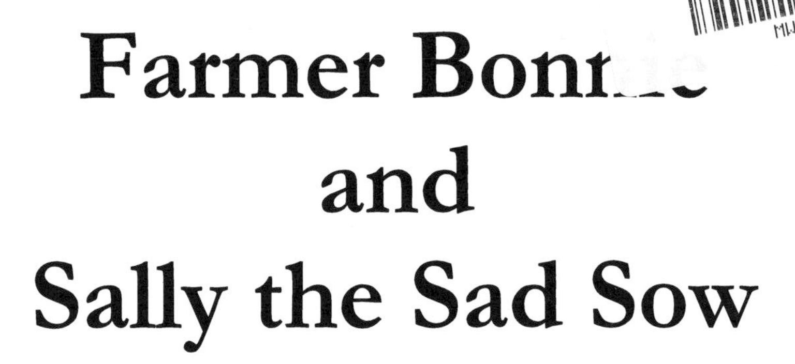

Farmer Bonnie and Sally the Sad Sow

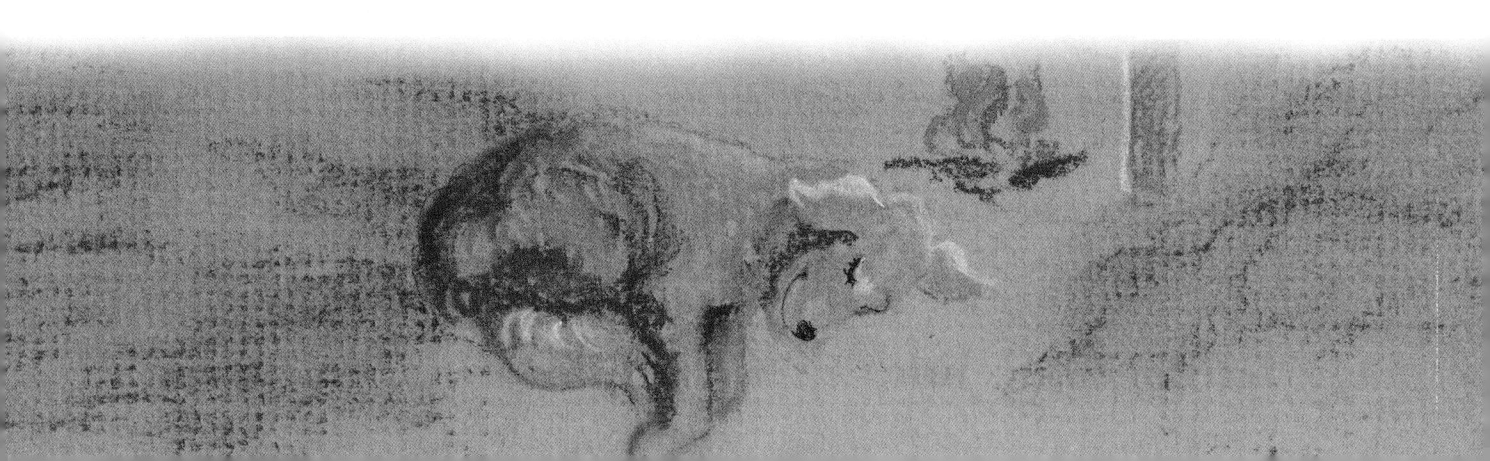

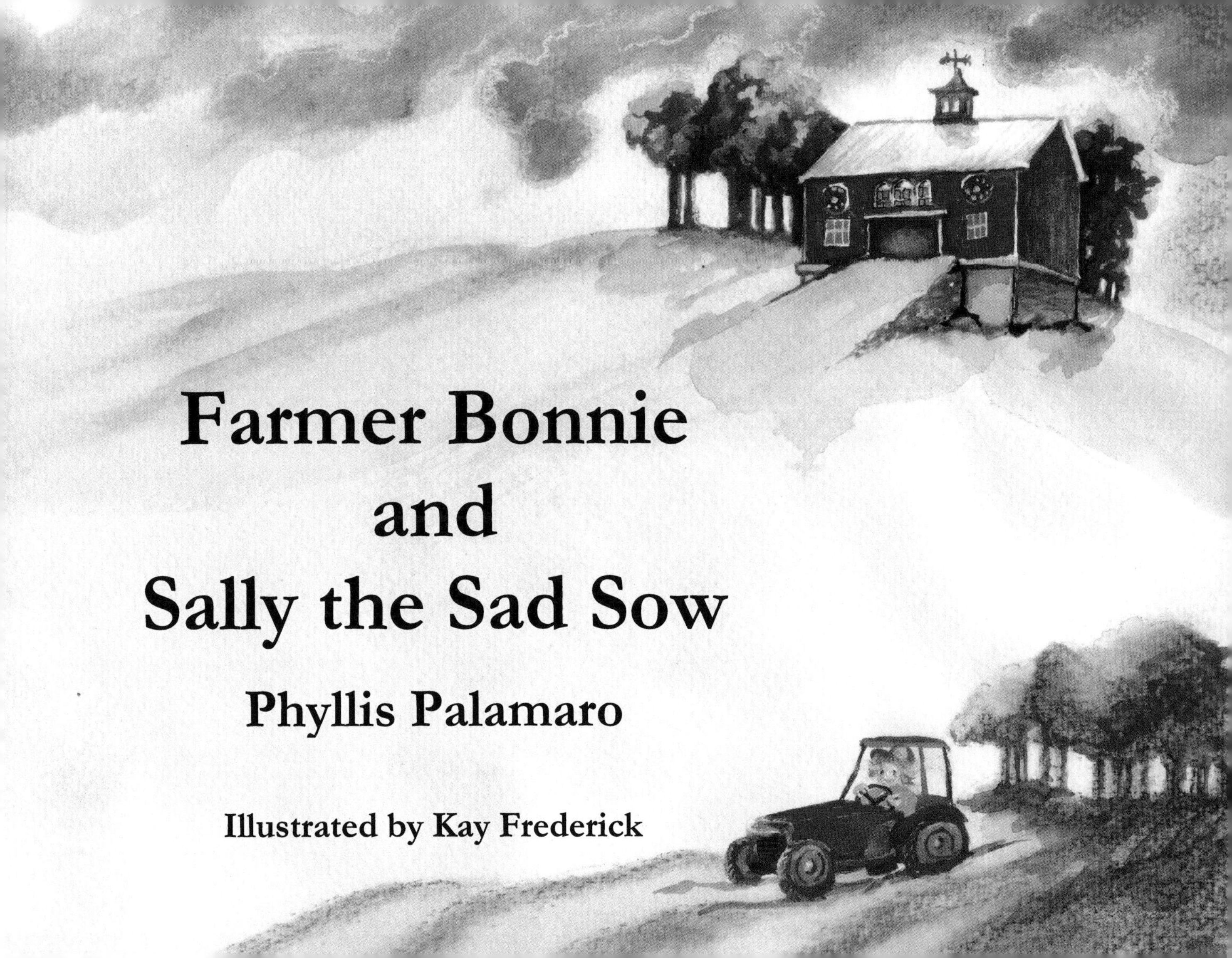

Farmer Bonnie and Sally the Sad Sow

Phyllis Palamaro

Illustrated by Kay Frederick

facebook.com/KayFrederickPaintings

Design and formatting by Bart Palamaro
indieauthorsupport.com

Dark Horse Productions, Bath PA 18014

ISBN-13: 978-1494324704
ISBN-10: 1494324709

DEDICATION

This book was written especially
for my friend Bonnie and
for children, young and old,
who have open hearts.

Sally lived on Farmer Bonnie's farm. She lived there many years, and was happy. Now she was sad.

Farmer Bonnie asked, "Why are you sad, Sally?"

Sally said, "I'm lonely."

Farmer Bonnie shook her head and said, "You have Sam the dog, the mules, the horse and the ducks."

"I know," said Sally, "but I'm still lonely."

Farmer Bonnie said,
"I'll ponder this in my
heart for awhile."

The next day Farmer Bonnie, Sally and Sam went to the Lehigh County Fair. On the way Sam said to Sally, "What's wrong?"

“I’m lonely,” said Sally. “Aren’t you, Sam?
You’re the only dog on the farm.”

"Heck no," said Sam. "I'm top dog here.

I can snooze by the fire, sit in Farmer Bonnie's lap and sleep on her bed. It's a perfect dog's life!"

At the fair, Sally won first prize for the sixth year in a row as the sleekest, most well groomed pig in the whole county.

Farmer Bonnie told Sally and Sam to behave as she went to fetch Sally's ribbon.

While she was gone Farmer Bonnie's best friend
Sarah passed them with Oscar, her pig.

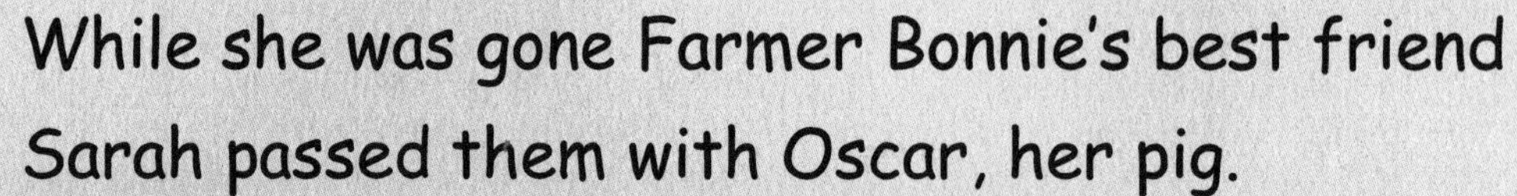

"Hi, guys. I need to find Oscar a new home. Do you think Farmer Bonnie might take him?"

"I don't know," said Sam. "But you could ask her. Here she comes."

As Farmer Bonnie returned she saw Sally gazing longingly at Oscar. "Ah ha! I think Sally's loneliness has been solved."

So Farmer Bonnie took
Oscar back to her farm.

Sally and Oscar had a big party for
their wedding at the farm.

Her friend Sarah came for
the happy occasion.

Sally and Oscar had three piglets, Bob, Brenda and Ben.

They all lived to a ripe old age, and none of them became bacon. Thank goodness!

Sam was an uncle to the piglets and kept them safe from cars and coyotes.

The moral of the story: "People and Pigs should not live alone."

ABOUT THE ILLUSTRATOR

A longtime overseas resident, artist/illustrator Kay recently returned to the Lehigh Valley. She received her BA from Lehigh University and her Masters in Illustration from Syracuse. Kay is on the board of the Lehigh Art Alliance, exhibits with the Paint Box Art Club of Nazareth and is a founding member of the Printmakers Society of the Lehigh Valley.

Kay aspires to help the reader step into Phyllis' charming world, characters and story. She uses Lehigh Valley vistas and images; a red barn and its neighboring fields of corn, a local artist's charming pig sculptures and the mallards of the Monocacy Creek. You may find the farm, fields and fairgrounds look familiar!

Thank you Phyllis and Bart for this inspiring journey to bring Phyllis' dream to fruition.

ABOUT THE AUTHOR

Phyllis has been an elementary school teacher most of her working life. She started in NYC, has taught in California and here in the Lehigh Valley. She has been a volunteer chaplain at Phoebe Home, Allentown for the past eight years. The thread that winds through both of these activities is storytelling. She loves to read and act out stories for children of all ages. Phyllis is Programs Chair of the Greater Lehigh Valley Writers Group, better known as GLVWG. GLVWG members encouraged her to write for Lilies of the Valley, the newsletter of the Parish Nurse Coalition of the Greater Lehigh Valley, where she is a contributing editor. Her passion is writing inspirational articles about God's hand in the different areas of her life.

ABOUT THE STORY

This story happened because of a phone company mistake. My friend Bonnie moved to another town, and had to change her phone number. The phone company got her name wrong and when she phoned, the Caller Id showed up as "Farmer Bonnie." We had a good laugh over that, when the Lord gave this idea to me. Thanks to my husband Bart, GLVWG critique groups, and illustrator Kay Frederick for making this story come to life.

Special thanks to Kay for her magnificent illustrations.

And very special thanks to Bart for hours of formatting the text, tweaking and "photoshopping" to make this book possible.

Phyllis Palamaro
November, 2013

Watch for

Farmer Bonnie
and
The Missing Mule

Coming in 2014